I Can Fly

Written by Michèle Dufresne

PIONEER VALLEY EDUCATIONAL PRESS, INC.

I am high
up in the sky.

I am a seagull
and I can fly.

I am high
up in the sky.

I am an eagle
and I can fly.

I am high
up in the sky.

I am a bluebird
and I can fly.

I am high
up in the sky.

I am an owl
and I can fly.

I am high
up in the sky.

I am a pelican
and I can fly.

I am high
up in the sky.

I am a crane
and I can fly.

I am high
up in the sky.

I am a goose
and I can fly.

I Can Fly

owl

eagle

bluebird

pelican

seagull

crane

goose